Raintree is an imprint of Capstone Global Library Limited, a
company incorporated in England and Wales having its registered
office at 264 Banbury Road, Oxford, OX2 7DY – Registered
company number: 6695582

www.raintree.co.uk
myorders@raintree.co.uk

Designed by Kay Fraser
Printed and bound in China

ISBN 978 1 3982 4142 8

British Library Cataloguing in Publication Data
A full catalogue record for this book is available from the British
Library.

CONTENTS

HARLEY QUINN'S™
MADCAP CAPERS

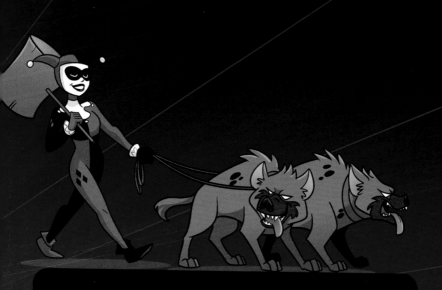

Dr Harleen Quinzel was once a successful psychiatrist at Gotham City's Arkham Asylum. But everything changed when she met the Joker. As the Clown Prince of Crime shared his heartbreaking — yet fake — story of a troubled childhood, Harleen's heart melted. She soon helped the Joker escape and joined him as a jolly jester with a calling for crime. Now she clowns around Gotham City, and these are . . .

HARLEY QUINN'S MADCAP CAPERS!

CHAPTER 1

Best burglar bet

Harleen Quinzel, better known to the people of Gotham City as Harley Quinn, had recently come into a large sum of money. To celebrate, she had invited Poison Ivy and Catwoman over to her apartment for brunch.

"The place looks perfect, Harls," said Catwoman. The cat burglar – whose secret identity was Selina Kyle – waved her hand around the room. "You sure can make a place your own."

Harley had used her new stash of cash to redecorate the dining room and living room of her huge loft apartment. It had fancy chandeliers, a new giant-screen TV and a dozen huge glass jars filled with bubble gum, sweets and chocolates.

Harley had even added a few touches for her friends. She had brought in lots of new plants to make Ivy feel comfortable. Then she had adopted just about every cat at the local animal shelter for Catwoman. Half a dozen of them now crawled over the feline felon as she lounged on the sofa like – well – a cat.

"Thanks, Cats. I wanted to make the place nice for my best girlfriends. You're both always welcome here." Harley glanced at Catwoman. "I mean, when I'm home. Not to, ya know, steal stuff."

Catwoman grinned.

"Why, Harley," the feline felon said, pressing her hand to her chest, "are you suggesting I'd steal from one of my dearest friends?"

"Are you suggesting you wouldn't, Selina?" Harley said in disbelief.

"Now, ladies, don't fight," Poison Ivy said. The red-haired villain – whose real name was Pamela Isley – paced among a trio of royal palms near the apartment's big picture window. Below in the distance, Arkham Asylum sat on an island in the Gotham River. "There is plenty of Gotham City for all of us and our particular styles."

"Exactly," Catwoman said. "My style just happens to be the best."

Harley stood over her, fists on hips. "Hey! I have loads of style. Mounds of it! Heaps!"

Ivy rolled her eyes.

"No one is saying you don't, Harleen," Catwoman said. "But my style almost never gets me caught. The two of you, on the other hand, are in and out of Arkham like it's got a revolving door."

"Ha!" Ivy said.

Harley and Catwoman looked at her. Ivy coughed and looked away.

"The reason," Harley said, returning her fiery glare to Catwoman, "that you're almost never caught is that Batman has a soft spot for you."

"Oh, please," Catwoman said. "I can easily handle Batman. Besides, having him wrapped around my little finger is all part of my skill set. It's why I'm the best burglar in the city – maybe even the best in the *world*."

"No way!" Harley replied.

"Harley," Ivy warned from among the vining houseplants that were twisting and climbing up the wrought-iron living room shelves. "Let it go."

Poison Ivy liked to stay close to the Green – the force that connected all plants in the world – and the vines liked having her near by too. They rubbed against her hands and legs like friendly cats.

"If Superman was in this city," Harley said, "or Wonder Woman, or heck, even Green Arrow, your burgling career would be shut down in one night."

"Goodness, Harley," Catwoman said. She slid across the sofa, scooped up two cats and curled up against an armrest. "You're so cute when you're jealous."

"Here we go," Ivy groaned.

"Jealous?!" Harley snarled. "That's it. I'm going to prove I'm as good at robbin' stuff as you. We'll make a bet."

"Oh, Harley," Ivy said with a sigh.

"What kind of bet?" Catwoman asked.

Harley looked around, trying to think of a contest. As she did, the TV showed a quick news story about an exhibit at the Gotham City Antiquities Gallery.

"The Marble of Atlantis was once believed to be nothing but a legend," said the reporter standing inside the gallery. "But now the massive pearl is on loan to the gallery and will debut tomorrow night at a very fancy and *very exclusive* black-tie event."

Harley's mouth dropped open. Ivy clicked off the TV.

"Harley," Ivy warned, "this is a bad idea."

"Is it, Pammy?" Harley asked. "Or is it the best idea I've ever had?"

"How long do I have to think about it?" Ivy replied sarcastically.

"I haven't heard any idea yet," said Catwoman.

"She's going to challenge you to a race to steal the Marble of Atlantis," Ivy said.

"Ivy!" Harley said. "I can speak for myself!"

She turned to Catwoman.

"I challenge you to a race to steal the Marble of Atlantis!" Harley shouted, thrusting one finger in the air.

"Challenge accepted," Catwoman said as she rose from the sofa.

"But there's more, Selina," Harley said. "I want Batman out of the picture until the challenge is over."

"Well, of course, darling," Catwoman said. She moved across the apartment, letting her fingertips run over the lids of the sweet jars. "That's the whole trick, isn't it? So, it's a lucky coincidence that Gotham City's own Caped Crusader will be out of town tomorrow night."

"Perfect!" Harley said. Then she narrowed her eyes at Catwoman. "Wait a sec. How do you know that?"

"I have kittens all over this city, Harls," Catwoman said. "You know that. And they come by my place and whisper in my ear. Lately they whispered to me about a major plot going down in Star City. Batman will have to respond."

"Something smells fishy, Harley," Ivy warned again as she took Catwoman's spot on the sofa. The cats hissed and hurried away from her.

"I can take care of myself, Red," Harley snarled. "It's a bet. Tomorrow night." She put out her hand to shake on it.

Catwoman's lips curled into a cunning smile as she gently took Harley's hand and shook it once. "You're on."

CHAPTER 2

Contests gotta have rules!

The next evening, as the sun went down, Harley Quinn was zonked out. Flanked by her pet hyenas, Crackers and Giggles, she was snoring the afternoon away when her apartment buzzer suddenly went off.

BZZZT! BZZZT!

"Come on, Ma!" Harley called out in her sleep. "Lemme sleep a few more minutes."

BZZZT! BZZZZZZT!

The buzzer rang again, louder this time and for what felt like hours.

Harley sat up and shoved off the blanket. Crackers and Giggles pushed her off the bed. Then the two hyenas curled up together and went back to sleep.

"I'm coming! I'm coming!" Harley shouted, annoyed by the rude awakening. She slammed her index finger against the answer button. "Who is it?!"

"It's Ivy, Harley," replied her best friend. From her tone, Harley could tell something was wrong. "Did you oversleep?"

"Oversleep?" Harley muttered to herself. She tried to remember what she'd done so far that day, but nothing came to mind. "I'm not sure. I just woke up. Did I miss something?"

"Not yet," Ivy said. "But you're about to. Buzz me in, okay?"

Harley shrugged, buzzed Ivy into the apartment building, and threw on her jester outfit. Dressed for lawbreaking, she winked at herself in the mirror and then threw open the front door to her apartment. Ivy was already standing there, about to knock.

"Oh good," Ivy said. "You're ready. Better get moving."

"Right!" Harley said. She grabbed her mallet from its leaning spot next to the door. "What's the heist, Red? We bustin' up some chemical companies for pollutin' a swamp?"

"What?" Ivy said.

"Let's see . . . we're blowin' up timber haulage for destroying an old-growth forest?" Harley tried.

"No," Ivy said, rolling her eyes. "Harley –"

"Wait, don't tell me," Harley said. "I'll remember. We're, uh, beating up some, um, stockholders for investing in . . . fossil fuels?"

"*I'm* not doing anything, Harls," Ivy said. "You, however, have a bet with Selina Kyle?"

"A bet . . . ," Harley mumbled.

"With Catwoman?" Ivy said. "To steal the huge pearl?"

Harley's eyes went wide. "The bet!" she shrieked. "I forgot! Did I miss it?" Harley ran through the apartment. "Where's my phone? What time is it?"

"It's almost six o'clock," Ivy said. "Selina tried calling you, but you didn't answer, so she called me. I presumed you'd be sleeping the day away with the hyenas still, so . . ."

"So here you are," Harley said as she dug through the sofa cushions. "My best friend who would do anything for me."

"Well, I don't know about *anything*," Ivy said. She slipped into the kitchen and grabbed Harley's phone off the worktop. When she walked back into the living room, Harley was sifting through dirty dishes on the coffee table. "Here's your phone, Harley."

"Thanks, Red," she said. She tapped the screen. A few moments later, Catwoman's masked face appeared, grinning like she'd swallowed a canary.

"Well, good morning, Harley," Catwoman said. "Or should I say 'good evening'?"

"Alright, alright," Harley said. "I'm up. I'm not the type of girl who usually keeps a schedule. So what?"

"So, our bet is about to begin," Catwoman said. "I decided to give you a fighting chance and help you wake up. But from here on out, you're on your own."

"No problem," Harley said, sneering at the screen. "I got this one in the bag. What are the rules?"

"Rules?" Catwoman said. She laughed lightly. "Darling, burglars don't follow rules."

"No honour among thieves, Harley," Ivy reminded her.

"This is a contest," Harley said. "Contests gotta have rules or it's just anarchy."

"I thought you liked anarchy," Ivy whispered. Harley shushed her.

"Here's what I say," Harley said. "No help from friends or sidekicks or street kittens or whatever."

"Or hyenas," Catwoman said. "Or former partners in crime."

"She means the Joker," Ivy whispered.

"I know who she means!" Harley snapped. "Fine," she added to the screen.

"Are you at your apartment?" Catwoman asked.

"Yup," Harley said. "Almost the exact same distance from the gallery as your place, but in the opposite direction."

"Perfect," Catwoman said. "We leave at six o'clock, and whoever steals the Marble of Atlantis has to bring it home to win."

"Better yet," Harley said, "the person who nabs that big, ol' pearl has to bring it to the other person's apartment."

"Ooh, I like it," Catwoman said. "I'm in."

"Great," Harley said. "And what does the winner get?"

Catwoman sighed. "You mean aside from the most valuable pearl the world has ever known?"

"Yeah," Harley said. "Aside from that. The loser has to give up something, right?"

Catwoman rolled her eyes.

"How about," Harley said, "the loser cooks breakfast for the winner for a week."

"Breakfast?" Catwoman said. "Darling, I'd be surprised if you ever woke up before dinner."

"I'll be up if you're cookin' for me!" Harley said.

"Fine," Catwoman said.

A gold clock behind Catwoman started to chime. After the sixth chime, it finally fell silent.

"Oh, look at the time," the feline felon said. "It's six. Break a leg, Dr Quinzel." The screen flashed red and went black.

"The race is on!" Harley announced.

"I bet she already has the pearl," Ivy said.

"Aw, don't be such a sourpuss," Harley said. She threw her arms around Ivy. "Wish me luck."

"Good luck," Ivy replied.

Harley ran to the window, threw it open and dived out headfirst.

"Harley!" Ivy shouted after her. "This is *your* apartment! You can use the front door!"

CHAPTER 3

Crosstown chaos

For Harley Quinn, jumping out of her apartment window was no big deal – she'd done it dozens of times. She swung from a fire escape, slid down an air-conditioning duct, wall-ran to the top of a third-floor balcony and bounded to the ground. She rolled into her landing in the alley behind her apartment building and quickly leaped to her feet.

"Darn," she said. "I forgot my mallet."

Harley looked up the side of the building towards her top-floor apartment. "No time for that now," she muttered. "Gotta move fast."

Harley Quinn was a lot of things: a former psychiatrist, a criminal mastermind, a championship gymnast and the life of the party. But she wasn't much of a car person. Harley usually liked to take the underground, buses and bicycles to get around the city. But those three options would take too long to get her to the gallery.

What she needed this evening was speed. And speed happened to be parked right beside her. A racing motorbike, with a helmet tucked behind the seat and the keys in the ignition, was parked in the alley.

"Must be some delivery person's bike," she said. "They're probably inside dropping off a parcel or a pizza right now."

With a shrug, Harley put on the helmet and climbed on. Thinking quickly, she rummaged through the bike's saddlebag and found a pen and a delivery receipt. On the back of the receipt she wrote: *Thanks for letting me borrow your bike. It's an emergency.*

Then Harley chewed a piece of gum, pulled it out and used it to stick the note to the wall.

"*Emergency,*" she told herself, "is a relative term." She turned the key, and the bike revved to life.

VROOOOM! Harley zoomed off, but she didn't get far.

Just a couple of blocks from her building, she screeched to a halt behind a big traffic jam.

"Move it, you bunch of bums!" she shouted while honking the bike's horn.

But it was no use. At the crossroads ahead, traffic was stopped dead. Craning her neck to see over the cars in front of her, Harley watched the light turn from green to red and back again. No one moved an inch.

"Arggh!" she snarled as she got off the bike, pulled off the helmet and ran.

"Super-Villain comin' through!" she shouted as she weaved between taxis and moving vans.

But when Harley finally reached the crossroads, she skidded on her heels. Right in the middle of it – as if it was their living room – were no fewer than fifty cats. Some played and rolled around. Others lounged and napped on the warm pavement.

"That low-down, dirty –" Harley pulled out her phone and tapped the screen. A minute later, Catwoman's face appeared.

"Hi, Harley," the cat burglar said. Harley squinted at the screen, but she couldn't tell where Catwoman was or how close she might be to the gallery by now.

"I said no pets!" Harley shouted into the phone. "I even said no cats!"

"What are you talking about, dear?" Catwoman said.

"I think you know," Harley replied.

"Why, Harley," Catwoman said, "I haven't the foggiest." Then Harley's screen went black. The villain had hung up.

"Grrrr!" Harley said with a stamp of her foot. But she couldn't give up now. Just past the crossroads, the traffic was clear.

Harley ran through the pile of cats, sending the felines scattering and hissing. Up ahead, a double-decker tour bus was parked along the kerb. With a leap, she climbed aboard just as the bus pulled away – slowly.

"Up on our right, you'll see the Church of Saint Helena," the driver announced over the loudspeaker. "It was moved to Gotham City from its original site in Europe and is famous for its stained-glass windows."

The bus lurched on at a crawl as cars zoomed past on both sides.

"This is very exciting," the driver said, though he didn't sound the least bit excited about it. "On our left is the oldest postbox in Gotham City."

Tourists leaned out the windows, taking photos.

"Ah," the driver said as the bus inched forwards, "now on the right, there's Twelfth National Bank. Aside from being the eleventh-oldest bank in Gotham City, there's nothing that interesting about it."

"Nothing interesting?!" Harley shouted. "That's it, buster. I'm takin' over!"

Harley grabbed the driver by the shirt and threw him out the bus door.

"I'll give you 'interesting,'" she said as she pulled on the driver's headset microphone. "The Twelfth National Bank was made internationally famous just last week when master criminal Harley Quinn knocked it over for a million bucks!" She slammed her foot against the accelerator. "Now let's get this tour into high gear!"

Harley tore along the streets. As she swerved around the other cars, the double-decker bus rocked from side to side.

She took a sharp left-turn at high speed. The tourists all screamed.

AAAAAHHHHH!!

"Hold on tight, folks," she announced. "This tour is finally gonna get really interesting!"

The bus sped along the avenue.

"On your left, that's one of Hugo Strange's secret labs!" Harley announced. "Harley Quinn and her bestie, Poison Ivy, freed two hundred poor monkeys from there before Strange could do any of his nasty experiments on 'em."

Cameras snapped, and tourists oohed and aahed as the bus sped on.

"Up here on your right," Harley said, "is where the Scarecrow dropped his fear gas on an entire police headquarters! That was a pretty exciting Sunday morning, as you can imagine."

It was much darker now. The streetlights were on, and, up ahead, waving spotlights and a line of headlights marked the location of a fancy, red-carpet, black-tie event.

"Well, well," Harley announced. "And finally, up ahead, is the world-famous Gotham City Antiquities Gallery! It's where none other than Harley Quinn herself – who none of you have seen in the area, if anyone asks – will steal the Marble of Atlantis tonight!"

Harley slammed on the brakes.

 SCREECH!

The bus skidded to a stop at the kerb, blocking in ten fancy limos and sports cars.

"Enjoy the rest of your tour," Harley announced as she leaped off the bus. "One of you will have to drive, I guess."

At the last moment, she leaned back onto the bus and grabbed a dry-cleaning bag hanging near the front seats.

"I'm just gonna borrow this too," she said to the young woman sitting in the front seat. "Thanks."

* * *

After a quick change in the garden outside the gallery, Harley – now in a fancy black and red dress, compliments of the stranger on the bus – strolled straight up to the front door.

"Name?" asked the big bouncer. He wore a black suit and black sunglasses. Although he only held a clipboard, the other two bouncers with him made getting into the gallery impossible.

"Doctor Harleen Quinzel," Harley said, lifting her chin. "I'm a well-regarded psychiatrist."

"Well regarded, huh?" the bouncer said as he scanned the list. "Not well-listed, though. You're not on here."

"Did you look under Q for *Quinzel*?" Harley asked.

"No," the bouncer said. "I looked under G for 'get lost'."

Harley opened her mouth to reply when she was shoved aside.

"Excuse me, dear," said a familiar voice.

"Selina?!" Harley snapped.

"I'm sorry, do I know you?" Selina said. She winked. She wore a shimmering black dress, a silver necklace and glittery diamond earrings.

"Evening, Miss Kyle," the bouncer said. He smiled and didn't even check the list. "You can go on in."

"Why, thank you so much, Martin," Selina said. She headed inside, but Harley grabbed her wrist.

"*Friend* of yours, Selina?" Harley snarled at her quietly.

Selina pulled her hand away as her face flashed with anger. "Don't make a scene, Harley, or you'll blow the whole thing."

Selina went in, and the three huge bouncers blocked the entrance again.

"Darn it, Selina!" Harley shouted after the villain. But it was no use. The bouncers blocked her view of the inside of the gallery, and there was no getting past them. She'd have to find another way in.

"Just act natural, Harley," she said to herself as she turned and strolled along a path that circled the gallery. A few other guests, all wearing smart clothes and sipping drinks, strolled there as well.

Harley smiled at them as she passed. "Beautiful night for it," she said cheerily.

At the back of the building, out of the lights of the path and garden, Harley found the service door. She tried the handle.

"Locked," she muttered. "Catwoman would have no problem picking that lock, I bet." Unfortunately, she didn't have a pick.

"And I forgot my mallet," Harley added sadly, "so I can't bash it in."

But then another door caught her eye. Just a few paces away was the groundskeeper's shed – and its door was unlocked!

Harley turned the handle and stepped into the dusty, musty-smelling shack. Almost instantly, she spotted a beam of light from a nearby lamppost shining through a crack in the roof. Even better, it illuminated the most beautiful thing Harley had ever seen.

"Can I be this lucky?" she squealed, placing her hands on her cheeks. Sitting in the beam of light – as if a gift from the heavens – was a huge wooden mallet.

Harley grabbed the mallet. Her hands fitted around the handle as if it had been made for her.

"This little contest is about to get really interesting," she said. Then she walked up to the service door and raised the mallet.

"Batter up!" Harley called as she started to swing.

"Wait a sec," she said, stopping her swing. "You wouldn't say 'batter up!' with a mallet." She rested the mallet's head on the ground and leaned on the handle. "Maybe 'look out below'? Nah, that's for jumping off stuff . . ."

She tapped her chin. "Ooh, I've got it!" she said.

Harley raised the mallet again and shouted, "I've got a hammer, and you look like a nail!"

WHAM! Harley slammed the mallet into the service door. It flew off its hinges, and shards of wood scattered in every direction.

Just inside the doorway sat a security guard. He had a half-eaten sandwich in his mouth and a comic book in one hand.

"Um," he said with the sandwich in his teeth. "Hello?"

"Hiya!" Harley said, stepping inside and kicking aside some debris. "Don't mind me. Just here to rob the place. It's all very official."

The guard looked her up and down, noting the giant mallet, the bits of door on the floor and the maniacal smile on her face. "I see," he said. "I'll just go on my break now."

"Thanks, mister!" Harley called after him as he hurried away. And with that, she dropped the mallet in the caretaker's cupboard and slipped into the party.

CHAPTER 4

The crooked kitty

The Antiquities Gallery had once been
a fancy mansion. Its massive front atrium
now served as the gallery's main hall – and
tonight it was decked out. White tablecloths
draped dozens of tall tables. Beautiful flowers
lined the central staircase. Gold and silver
streamers adorned the chandeliers. And, to
top it all off, a large banner that read, *The
Marble of Atlantis – The World's Most Exquisite
Treasure* hung below the hall's huge skylight.

Harley watched as dozens of waiters and waitresses weaved through the gathered guests with trays loaded with drinks and nibbles. As one passed, she grabbed a mini-quiche and wandered towards the back of the hall. There, a spotlight shone down on a stone pedestal. A blue cloth covered the top of the pedestal, blocking the evening's star – the Marble of Atlantis – from view. A pair of guards stood on either side of the display.

"So," Harley said, strolling up to them, "when's the unveiling tonight?"

"In just a few minutes," one of the guards said. He held up one palm. "You better take a few steps back, though, Miss. We don't want to have to move you back by force."

"I appreciate that, big guy!" Harley said, saluting. She stepped back a bit and studied the situation.

Getting past these two will be impossible, Harley thought. *I'll have to distract them somehow, or approach the pedestal from the back. If I could get behind there, by cutting all the power so the lights went off, maybe –*

"Welcome to the Gotham City Antiquities Gallery!" a voice boomed from the speakers lining the hall.

Harley spun around. She spotted the gallery's curator at the top of the staircase. He held a microphone in his hand.

"Thank you so much for coming out tonight," he said, "and for your generous donations throughout the year. Without the support of Gotham City's finest, we would never have attracted a donation like the one we're prepared to share tonight."

CLAP! CLAP! CLAP! CLAP!

"Which, of course, is why you're all here tonight," the man continued. "So, without further ado, let me introduce the generous woman who donated the beautiful prize for this two-month exhibit." He turned and raised his hand to a hallway out of sight. "Miss Selina Kyle!"

Harley nearly fell over as Selina strolled up to the man, gave him a kiss on the cheek, and took the microphone.

"Friends of the gallery," Selina said, "I'm so pleased you could all be here this evening." As she spoke, she walked slowly and gracefully down the grand staircase. "The Marble of Atlantis all but fell into my possession a few short weeks ago."

"'Fell' my foot!" Harley mumbled, crossing her arms.

Selina reached the bottom of the stairs and approached the stone pillar. "My first thought upon holding the massive pearl was, *Oh my, this is a beautiful item.*" Selina paused, and the crowd laughed and clapped. "Then I thought, *I simply must donate this to the Antiquities Gallery.* After all, this place has meant so much to me. In fact, it has given me more than I could ever truly repay."

Selina grabbed the golden tassel that hung next to the blue cloth. The lights in the hall dimmed.

"I'm so thrilled to introduce all of you to the long lost . . ." Selina pulled the tassel, and the cloth flew up to the ceiling. "Marble of Atlantis!"

There it was – a pearl as big as a basketball – shining in the spotlight. And Selina simply reached over and picked it up.

Harley backed her way through the crowd and dropped onto a bench at the bottom of the stairs. Her dress poofed up around her.

"Darn it," she said, leaning her chin on her fists. She stopped listening to the speech, and after a while the murmur of conversation and clinking glasses returned.

Soon, Selina walked over and sat next to Harley.

"You cheated," Harley said. "The pearl was yours the whole time. This was never a competition at all."

"Oh, Harley," Selina said. "Of course, I cheated. It's what I do. It's what *we* do, or have you forgotten?"

Harley leaned back against the cold wall and crossed her arms. "Forgotten what?" she asked.

"That we're the bad guys, silly," Selina said, nodding towards the pedestal, where the pearl once again sat protected by the guards. "I stole the Marble weeks ago."

"And set me up to look ridiculous," Harley added.

"Now, Harley," Selina said. "You set yourself up. I told you I was the best burglar in the biz, and maybe next time you won't mess with me." She stood up. "I was going to get you thrown out, but I don't have the heart. Enjoy the rest of the party."

With that, Selina walked up the stairs.

Harley leaned her head back and stared out of the skylight in the ceiling. Through it she saw the full moon shining brightly, and that gave her an idea.

Maybe this contest wasn't over after all.

CHAPTER 5

Best in jest

Long into the night, Selina mingled with Gotham City's richest people. None of them knew she was really Catwoman. None of them knew this party was little more than a celebration for the best burglar in the world.

But Harley knew as she looked down at the glamorous thief through the skylight on the roof. She was back in her jester costume now, and the borrowed dress was stuck in the gallery's lost and found box.

Harley pulled out her phone and dialled her frenemy.

"Hiya, Cats," she said. "How's the party going in there?"

"Harley," Selina replied. Harley watched her move away from the crowd of admirers. "Have you left already?"

"Yeah," Harley said. "You know me. I just can't stand these highfalutin functions. Full of fake people and stuck-up posers. But listen, I was thinkin' . . ."

"Careful, Harley," Selina said, "don't strain yourself."

"If you stole the Marble of Atlantis weeks ago and all," Harley went on, "I guess Batman and the Justice League and all those do-gooder capes must still be lookin' for it, ain't that right?"

"I suppose so," Selina said. "So what? I told you, Batman is out of town tonight."

"You sure about that?" Harley asked. "I'd look up at the skylight if I was you."

She watched as Selina lowered her phone and looked up at the skylight. The full moon shone through the window – but its light was broken up by the familiar silhouette of the Caped Crusader looking down at her.

"Batman!" Selina gasped into the phone. "But . . . how?"

"I know, right?" Harley said. "I guess he's on to you. You better scram."

Selina hung up. Then she whispered something to the guards at the pedestal and reached to grab the Marble. But she stopped when she noticed the gallery's curator standing right next to it.

Quickly, Selina and the two guards fled the party, leaving the marble behind.

"It worked!" Harley said. She lowered her prop and spread it on the rooftop to admire her handiwork.

Her creation was made from odds and ends she'd found in the gallery's back room: an old, tattered curtain, a curtain rod, a couple of coat hangers wrapped in paper and, of course, the big mallet to hold it all up. Cobbled together, her little invention had made a perfect Batman silhouette in the moonlight.

"The rest of my plan should be a piece of cake," Harley said to herself. Then she grabbed the mallet and slammed it against the rooftop air-conditioning unit.

WHACK! FZZZZT!

The unit popped and crackled before finally going *BOOM!* The explosion rocked the building and cut out all the electricity in the process.

Then Harley popped open a window in the skylight and leaped onto the huge banner hanging over the hall.

WHOOSH!

She swung down into the pitch-black room with her mallet in one hand. Near the floor, she released the banner and landed next to the Marble of Atlantis and the curator.

"This was a great party," Harley said, patting the man on his head. "Give my regards to Selina when you see her, okay?"

"Who's there?" the curator said. "Stand back! I'm warning you. I'm trained in several forms of self-defence!"

"Sure ya are," Harley said, grabbing the pearl. "I bet that'll come in handy for you one day. But I'm holding a mallet bigger than you, so probably don't try anything. Enjoy the rest of the evening!"

She walked quickly from the room, her mallet over her shoulder and the pearl tucked under one arm like a football. Thanks to the darkness and the chaos in the room, no one even saw her leave.

* * *

As the sun began to rise over Gotham City's skyline, Harley sat on a sofa inside a quiet apartment. She was surrounded by cats, and the Marble of Atlantis rested on the cushion beside her. She used a remote to flick through TV channels as she waited.

Suddenly the apartment door opened, and Selina Kyle walked in. She looked very, very tired.

"Jeez, Cats, you musta been running all night!" Harley said. "Did Bats finally catch up with ya?"

"Harley!" Catwoman said. "What are you doing here?"

"Don't ya remember our bet?" Harley asked. "Whichever of us grabbed the Marble of Atlantis and brought it back to the other's apartment was the winner, right?" She lifted the pearl with both hands over her head. "Well, here it is, and here I am – in *your* apartment."

"But . . . that's impossible," Catwoman said. "Batman was there. How did you get past him?"

"B-man was there?" Harley said, laying the Marble back down on the sofa cushion. "I guess we must have just missed each other. Oh, wait a sec." She nodded at the TV and clicked the remote. On the screen, a news network featured a story that had been unfolding all night.

"Latest reports indicate Star City nearly fell victim to a poison attack by a group of Super-Villains from Gotham City, Metropolis, and Star City itself," the news reporter said. "But eyewitnesses say Green Arrow, Superman and Batman were all spotted in the city to foil the plot."

"How about that. I guess Bats wasn't at the gallery at all," Harley said, barely containing her laughter.

"But . . . ," Catwoman said, "I saw him. I know I saw him!"

"Sorry, Cats," Harley said. "You lost, fair and square."

"Fair and square," Catwoman repeated softly as she dropped onto the sofa. The Marble of Atlantis bounced and rolled up against her thigh.

"Don't sit down," Harley said as she aimed the remote and flicked to a cartoon channel. "Sun's comin' up, and I want breakfast. Make it an egg and cheese sandwich with extra bacon. And coffee with lots of cream and sugar."

GRRR! Catwoman growled as she got up and trudged towards the kitchen.

"Aw, heck, make it two sandwiches," Harley called out with a giggle. "It was a long night, and I'm starvin'!"

CATWOMAN

REAL NAME: Selina Kyle
OCCUPATION: Professional thief
BASE: Gotham City

BIOGRAPHY: Much like Gotham City's famous billionaire, Bruce Wayne, Selina Kyle was orphaned at a young age. But unlike Bruce, Selina had no caretakers or family fortune to support her. Growing up alone on the mean streets of Gotham City, Selina was forced to resort to petty crime in order to survive. Soon, she was one of the city's most dangerous criminals. Becoming Catwoman to hide her true identity, Selina now prowls the streets, preying on the wealthy while guarding Gotham City's fellow castaways.

HARLEY'S FRIENDS AND FOES

FRIENDS

Harley & Poison Ivy

Harley & The Joker

Catwoman

Giggles, Harley & Crackers

FOES

Batman

Robin

Batgirl

Batwoman

Batwing

BIOGRAPHIES

photo by Andrew Karre

STEVE BREZENOFF is the author of more than fifty chapter books, including the Field Trip Mysteries series, the Ravens Pass series of thrillers and the Return to the Titanic series. He's also written three YA novels, *Guy in Real Life; Brooklyn, Burning* and *The Absolute Value of -1*. In his spare time, he enjoys video games, cycling and cooking. Steve lives in Minneapolis, USA, with his wife, Beth, and their son and daughter.

illustration by Sarah Leuver

SARAH LEUVER is a comic artist who who has worked on series such as Teen Titans Go! and DC Superhero Girls. When she's not drawing super heroes for work, she can usually be found drawing them for fun. She lives in San Francisco Bay, USA. When she isn't drawing, she enjoys spending time with her family and her dog, Oliver.

anarchy situation with no order and no one in control

antiquities objects from an earlier time

atrium patio or courtyard around which a building is built

bouncer security guard at an event

chandelier light fixture that hangs from the ceiling

curator person in charge of a place that displays exhibits

debut first showing

exquisite very beautiful and delicate

felon criminal convicted of severe crimes

hyena wild animal that looks somewhat like a dog

psychiatrist medical doctor who is trained to treat
emotional issues and mental illness

silhouette outline of something that shows its shape

TALK ABOUT IT

1. Harley makes a bet with Catwoman to determine who is the best burglar. Think of a time you made a bet with a friend or family member. What did you bet on? Did you win or lose?

2. What do you think would have happened if Poison Ivy had joined the bet with Harley and Catwoman? Who do you think would have won the contest, and why?

3. Harley tricks Catwoman into believing Batman has arrived at the gallery. How else might she have chased the feline felon away and stolen the pearl?

WRITE ABOUT IT

1. Harley's apartment has recently been redecorated at the start of the story. If you could redecorate your room, what would you change? Make a list of fun things you would add. Then draw a picture of what your redecorated room would look like.

2. Harley believes contests must have rules. Catwoman disagrees because they are both criminals. Who do you believe is right? Write a paragraph that explains what you think, and why.

3. At the end of the story, Harley wins the bet and Catwoman has to make her breakfast. Write a new chapter about what happens next. Does Catwoman turn out to be a good cook or a rubbish one? You decide!

READ THEM ALL!

The Harley and Batgirl Show

by Michael Anthony Steele illustrated by Sarah Leuver

Catwoman's Crooked Contest

by Steve Brezenoff illustrated by Sarah Leuver

Poison Ivy's Big Boss in Bloom

by Michael Anthony Steele illustrated by Sara Foresti

The Joker Hideout Heist

by Steve Brezenoff illustrated by Sara Foresti

FROM RAINTREE